Dear Parents and Educators,

Welcome to Penguin Young Readers! As parents and educators, you know that each child develops at his or her own pace—in terms of speech, critical thinking, and, of course, reading. Penguin Young Readers recognizes this fact. As a result, each Penguin Young Readers book is assigned a traditional easy-to-read level (1–4) as well as a Guided Reading Level (A–P). Both of these systems will help you choose the right book for your child. Please refer to the back of each book for specific leveling information. Penguin Young Readers features esteemed authors and illustrators, stories about favorite characters, fascinating nonfiction, and more!

Bones and the Apple Pie Mystery

LEVEL **3**

GUIDED READING -LEVEL **J**

This book is perfect for a **Transitional Reader** who:
- can read multisyllable and compound words;
- can read words with prefixes and suffixes;
- is able to identify story elements (beginning, middle, end, plot, setting, characters, problem, solution); and
- can understand different points of view.

Here are some **activities** you can do during and after reading this book:
- Making Connections: Grandpa has a favorite fork he loves so much he brought it to Sally's house. Do you have a favorite object, such as a stuffed animal, toy, or article of clothing? Discuss how that object helps make activities even more special.
- Creative Writing: Imagine a day at the county fair. What would you do and which booths might you visit? Would you taste Sally's apple pie or another type of pie? Write a paragraph about all the things you would see and do!

Remember, sharing the love of reading with a child is the best gift you can give!

—Bonnie Bader, EdM
   Penguin Young Readers program

*Penguin Young Readers are leveled by independent reviewers applying the standards developed by Irene Fountas and Gay Su Pinnell in *Matching Books to Readers: Using Leveled Books in Guided Reading*, Heinemann, 1999.

For Natalie and Ivy Zellner—DAA

For my grandmother June, who taught me
how to bake lots of things, including pies!
—BJN

PENGUIN YOUNG READERS
Published by the Penguin Group
Penguin Group (USA) LLC, 375 Hudson Street, New York, New York 10014, USA

USA | Canada | UK | Ireland | Australia | New Zealand | India | South Africa | China

penguin.com
A Penguin Random House Company

Text copyright © 2013 by David A. Adler. Illustrations copyright © 2013 by Barbara Johansen Newman.
All rights reserved. Previously published in hardcover in 2013 by Penguin Young Readers.
This paperback edition published in 2014 by Penguin Young Readers, an imprint of
Penguin Group (USA) LLC, 345 Hudson Street, New York, New York 10014.
Manufactured in China.

The Library of Congress has cataloged the hardcover edition
under the following Control Number: 2012044874

ISBN 978-0-448-48231-6   10 9 8 7 6 5 4 3 2 1

BONES
and the Apple Pie Mystery

by David A. Adler
illustrated by Barbara Johansen Newman

Penguin Young Readers
An Imprint of Penguin Group (USA) LLC

Contents

Chapter 1
I'm Detective Jeffrey Bones

"We'll surprise Sally," Grandpa said,

"and maybe she'll surprise us."

Sally is Grandpa's friend.

Every year she tries to win the

Best Pie Contest at the county fair.

"She doesn't have a car,"

Grandpa said.

"We'll drive her to the fair."

Sally has a pie-baking trick.

Grandpa said, "She bakes two pies.

She puts one in the oven.

A few minutes later she puts the

second one in.

When the first one gets too crisp,

the second is just right."

Grandpa smiled.

"What do you think she'll do
with the crispy pie?"

I shook my head.

I didn't know.

"I think she'll let us eat the
crispy pie," Grandpa said.

Grandpa showed me his favorite fork.

It says *Max* on the handle.

That's Grandpa's name.

Grandpa brought his fork,

and I brought my detective bag.

I'm a famous detective.

I'm Detective Jeffrey Bones.

I find clues.

I solve mysteries.

Chapter 2
Busy Beth and Oliver

Grandpa knocked on Sally's door.

We waited.

Then Sally opened the door.

A large dog was with her.

The dog barked and jumped
on Grandpa.

"Get down, Oliver," Sally shouted.

"Get down!"

Oliver got down.

"Sit!" Sally told Oliver.

Oliver sat.

"Busy Beth is here," Sally said.

"She's my sister, and Oliver is her dog."

Grandpa said, "That's nice,

but we didn't come to see

Busy Beth and Oliver.

We came to help you bake apple pies."

Sally laughed.

"You don't know Beth," she said.

"Beth helped me make the dough.

She put the dough in pans,

cut the apples, filled the pies,

and put them in the oven.

She cleaned the kitchen, and

washed and ironed the aprons,

tablecloth, and towels."

Grandpa said, "I'm tired
just listening to all that."
I said, "Now I know why
you call her Busy Beth."
"Beth kept me so busy
I didn't watch the pies," Sally told us.
"The crust on the first pie
is much too crisp.
Would you help me eat it?"

"Sure," Grandpa said.

"I love crisp crust."

Grandpa took out his Max fork.

"Come with me," Sally said.

"The pies are on the kitchen table."

We followed Sally into the kitchen.

The table was there,

but the pies were gone.

Chapter 3
Ruff! Ruff!

"Are you sure you baked them today?" Grandpa asked.

"Of course I'm sure," Sally said.

I was sure, too.

I have a nose for clues,

and I could smell apple pie.

I had an idea.

"Maybe you left them in the oven,"
I said.

"No," Sally told me.

"I left them on the table."

Just to be sure, Grandpa opened

the oven.

"You're right," Grandpa said.

"The pies are not in here."

"Of course I'm right,"
Sally told him.

Ruff! Ruff!

Oliver ran into the kitchen
and jumped onto Grandpa.

Grandpa fell onto a chair.

Ruff! Ruff!

Oliver licked Grandpa's shirt.

Everyone likes Grandpa, even dogs.

And I know what Grandpa likes.

Grandpa likes apple pie.

Where were Sally's pies?

I looked under the table.

I looked on the counter.

I looked in the refrigerator, in the

freezer, and in the dish cabinet.

Then I looked at Oliver.

Oliver looked at me.

Ruff! Ruff!

"That's it," I said.

"I know what happened
to the apple pies.
Oliver ate them."

Chapter 4
I'll Find the Pies

I took my detective glass

out of my bag.

"I'm looking for pie crumbs," I said.

Grandpa held Oliver.

Dogs are messy eaters.

I looked for crumbs

in Oliver's doggy hairs.

I didn't find any.

"Oliver didn't eat the pies," I said.

"Of course he didn't," Sally told me.

"If he did, the pans would still
be here."

"Where's Busy Beth?" Grandpa
asked.

"She might know what happened
to the pies."

"I'm a detective.

I'll find Busy Beth," I said.

I looked in the hall.

I looked through my glass,

but I didn't find Busy Beth.

Grandpa, Sally, and Oliver

followed me.

Ruff! Ruff!

"Be quiet," Sally told Oliver.

I looked in the bathroom

and dining room.

Then I looked in the den.

Busy Beth was on the couch.

She was sleeping.

"Beth keeps busy," Sally said.

"Then she gets tired."

"Let's wake her and ask her about
the pies," Grandpa said.

"Don't wake Beth," I said.

"I'm a detective.

I'll find the pies."

"Please, hurry," Grandpa said,
waving his Max fork.

"I'm hungry."

Beth's things were in the den.

Near the couch was a small suitcase.

On the table were a purse

and a ring of keys.

Ruff! Ruff!

I looked at the keys

and I looked at Oliver.

Right then I knew

where to find the apple pies.

Chapter 5
First Prize

"What would you do," I asked,
"if you had a big dog and
two apple pies?"
Grandpa and Sally shook
their heads.
They didn't know.
"Look," I said, and pointed
to the keys.

"Those are not in Beth's purse because she just used them."

Ruff! Ruff!

Oliver's *Ruff! Ruff!* woke Busy Beth.

She rubbed her eyes.

"Hey," she said.

"Why are you watching me sleep?"

Sally told her, "We're looking for the pies."

"Oh," Beth said.

"I'll tell you where they are."

"Please, let me tell," I said.

"You put them in your car."

"Yes," Beth said.

"You didn't want Oliver to eat them."

"Yes," Beth said.

"I have dog food and biscuits
for Oliver.

The pies aren't for him.

Sally wants to take one pie to the

fair and one to her friend Max."

"Look," Grandpa said.

He showed Beth his fork.

"I'm Max."

"And I'm Jeffrey Bones," I said.

"I'm a detective.

I solve mysteries."

Beth sat up.

I said, "I just solved

the Apple Pie Mystery."

"That's nice," Busy Beth said.

I waited.

"I solve mysteries," I said,

"and I eat apple pie."

"Oh," Busy Beth said.

She took her keys, hurried to her car,

and brought back a large white box.

Max was written on the box.

We sat in the kitchen.

Busy Beth gave me a plate,

a fork, a napkin, and a slice of pie.

She gave Grandpa and Sally

pie, too.

Ruff! Ruff!

She gave Oliver a dog biscuit.

She got out a broom and waited.

"With crisp crust," she said,

"there are lots of crumbs."

We all tasted the pie.

"First prize!" Grandpa said.

Grandpa was right.

The pie was delicious.

Beth was also right.

There were lots of crumbs.

Busy Beth hurried and swept
them up.

I was right, too.

I knew what had happened
to Sally's pies.

I had solved the delicious,
crumbly apple pie mystery.